P9-EMP-507

Copyright © 1996 by Nord-Süd Verlag AG, Gossau Zürich, Switzerland.
First published in Switzerland under the title *Brüderchen und
Schwesterchen*. English translation copyright © 1996 by North-South
Books Inc. All rights reserved. No part of this book may be reproduced
or utilized in any form or by any means, electronic or mechanical,
including photocopying, recording, or any information storage and
retrieval system, without permission in writing from the publisher.

First published in the United States, Great Britain, Canada,
Australia, and New Zealand in 1996 by North-South Books,
an imprint of Nord-Süd Verlag AG, Gossau Zürich, Switzerland.
Distributed in the United States by North-South Books Inc., New York.

Library of Congress Cataloging-in-Publication Data is available.
A CIP catalogue record for this book is available from
The British Library.

ISBN 1-55858-588-5 (TRADE BINDING) 10 9 8 7 6 5 4 3 2 1
ISBN 1-55858-589-3 (LIBRARY BINDING) 10 9 8 7 6 5 4 3 2 1
Printed in Belgium

Little Brother and Little Sister

A Fairy Tale by Jacob and Wilhelm Grimm

Translated by Anthea Bell

Illustrated by Bernadette Watts

BROWNELL LIBRARY
HOME OF
LITTLE COMPTON
FREE PUBLIC LIBRARY

North-South Books

NEW YORK · LONDON

ONE DAY Little Brother took Little Sister's hand and said, "We've led a sad life since our mother died. Our stepmother beats us every day, and when we go near her she kicks us away. The only food we get is hard, stale bread crusts. Even the little dog under the table is better off—she throws him something nice to eat now and then. If only our mother knew! Come along, let's go out into the wide world to seek our fortune."

So they walked all day, over fields and meadows and rocks, and when it rained, Little Sister said, "God and our hearts are weeping together!"

That evening they came to a great forest, and they were so tired from their long journey that they settled down in a hollow tree and fell asleep.

When they woke up the next day, the sun was already standing high in the sky.
"Little Sister, I'm so thirsty," said Little Brother. "I think I hear the sound of
water somewhere. If I could find the stream, I'd drink from it."

Little Brother stood up and took Little Sister's hand, and they went in search of a stream. But their wicked stepmother was a witch. She had followed the two children in secret, as only witches can, and she had cast a spell on all the streams in the forest.

When the children came to a stream that sparkled as it flowed over its stony bed, Little Brother was about to drink from it. But Little Sister heard a voice in the water, and the voice said, "If you drink from me, a tiger you'll be; if you drink from me, a tiger you'll be."

"Please don't drink, Little Brother!" cried Little Sister. "If you do, you'll turn into a wild beast and tear me to pieces."

So although he was very thirsty, Little Brother didn't drink. "I'll wait until we find another stream," he said.

At the next little stream Little Sister heard another voice in the water, saying, "If you drink from me, a wolf you'll be; if you drink from me, a wolf you'll be."

"Oh, Little Brother, please don't drink!" cried Little Sister. "If you do, you'll turn into a wolf and eat me up."

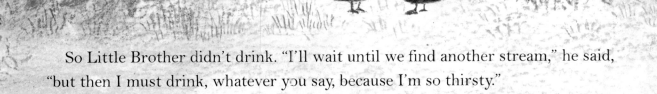

So Little Brother didn't drink. "I'll wait until we find another stream," he said,
"but then I must drink, whatever you say, because I'm so thirsty."

When they came to the third stream, Little Sister heard a voice in the water saying, "If you drink from me, a deer you'll be; if you drink from me, a deer you'll be."

"Oh, Little Brother, please don't drink!" said Little Sister. "If you do, you'll turn into a deer and run away from me."

But Little Brother had already knelt down by the stream, bent his head, and drunk from its water. As the first drops touched his lips, he turned into a little deer.

Little Sister wept bitterly over her poor bewitched brother, and the little deer wept too.

At last the girl said, "Hush, beloved little deer. I will never leave you."

Then she took off her golden garter and put it around the deer's neck. She picked some rushes and wove them into a soft cord, tied the little deer to this cord, and led him away, going deeper and deeper into the forest.

At last, when they had gone a long, long way, they came to a little house. The girl looked inside and saw that it was empty. We can live in this house, she thought. Then she collected leaves and moss to make the little deer a soft bed.

From then on the girl went out every morning, gathering roots, berries, and nuts for herself and bringing back tender grass for the deer. He ate it from her hand and played happily around her.

In the evening, after Little Sister had said her prayers, she would lay her head on the little deer's back as a pillow and sleep soundly. So they lived there alone in the forest for a long time, and if only Little Brother had been in human shape they would have been very happy.

One day the king of that country held a great hunt in the forest. The sound of horns, the barking of hounds, and the merry cries of the huntsmen echoed through the trees. Hearing it, the little deer longed to see the hunt for himself.

"Oh, do let me out to the hunt," he asked Little Sister. And he begged and begged until she agreed.

"But you must come back to me in the evening," she told him. "I'll keep my door shut for fear of the rough huntsmen, so let me know it's you by knocking and saying, 'Little Sister, let me in.' If you don't say that, I won't open the door."

BROWNELL LIBRARY
HOME OF
LITTLE COMPTON
FREE PUBLIC LIBRARY

The little deer leaped out of the house. He felt very merry in the open air. The king and his huntsmen saw the pretty animal and gave chase, but every time they were about to catch him, he bounded away through the bushes and disappeared.

When darkness fell, the deer ran back to the little house, knocked on the door, and said, "Little Sister, let me in."

The door opened, he went in, and he rested on his soft bed all night long.

The next morning the hunt began again, and once more the little deer
couldn't rest easy when he heard the hunting horn and the shouts of the huntsmen.
"Little Sister, open the door! I must go out," he said.

So Little Sister opened the door, saying, "But mind you're back by evening,
and don't forget the password."

When the king and his huntsmen saw the little deer with the golden collar
again, they all chased him, but he was too quick and nimble for them.

They hunted him all day long, and when evening began to fall, the huntsmen
had him surrounded. One of them wounded the little deer's foot slightly, making
him limp, so that he moved much more slowly as he ran away.

A huntsman followed him in secret to the little house and overheard him saying, "Little Sister, let me in." Then the huntsman saw the door open, and close again at once. He went back to the king and told him what he had seen and heard.

Little Sister was horrified to see that her little deer was wounded. She washed the blood away, put herbs on the wound, and said, "Go and lie down on your bed, my little deer."

However, the wound was so slight that the little deer was in no pain the next morning, and when he heard the huntsmen again, he said, "I can't bear it in here! I must go and see the hunt. They won't catch me again in a hurry."

Little Sister wept and said, "They'll kill you, and I'll be left all alone in the forest without another living soul. I won't let you out!"

"Then I will die of grief here," said the little deer. "When I hear the hunting horn, I just have to go out and run!"

Little Sister saw there was nothing else she could do, so with a heavy heart she opened the door for him, and the little deer ran happily into the forest, quite better again. When the king saw him, he told his huntsmen, "Hunt that deer all day long until nightfall, but make sure no one hurts him."

At sunset the king made the huntsman who had followed the deer show him the little house in the forest. When he came to the door, he knocked and called:

"Little Sister, let me in!" Then the door opened, and the king saw the most beautiful girl he had ever set eyes upon standing in the doorway.

The girl was afraid when she saw a man with a golden crown on his head instead of her little deer. But the king looked kindly at her, gave her his hand, and said, "Will you come to my castle with me, and be my dear wife?"

"Oh, yes," replied the girl, "but the deer must come with me. I cannot leave him."

"He can stay with you as long as you live, and he will want for nothing," said the king.

Just then the little deer came running in, and Little Sister tied him to one end of the cord of rushes. She held the other end, and they left the house in the forest together. The king put the beautiful girl on his horse and took her to his castle, where their wedding was celebrated with great magnificence. She was queen now, and she and the king lived happily together for a long time. The little deer was very well cared for, and played in the castle gardens.

Now the wicked stepmother, whose unkindness had sent the children out into the world in the first place, had expected Little Sister to be torn to pieces by wild beasts in the forest, and Little Brother, in the form of a young deer, to be shot by the huntsmen. When she heard that they were well and happy, jealousy stirred in her heart and gave her no peace. She did nothing all day but think how to harm them again.

Her own daughter, who was very ugly and had only one eye, was cross with her and said, "Why couldn't I be queen? I deserve it just as much!"

"Hush," said the old woman, soothing her. "I'll come up with a plan when the time is right."

Time went by, and the queen had a baby, a lovely little boy. The king was out hunting when the child was born. The wicked stepmother took the shape of a chambermaid, went into the room where the queen lay in bed, and told her, "Come along, your bath is ready. It will do you good and give you new strength, but hurry before it gets cold."

Her daughter was with her too, and between them they carried the queen, weak as she was, into the bathroom and put her in the tub. Then they locked the door and left. However, they had lit a blazing hot fire in the bathroom that suffocated the beautiful young queen.

The old witch then took her daughter, put a nightcap on her head, and told her to get into the queen's bed. She made her look like the queen in face and figure, too, except for the missing eye. She couldn't do anything about that, so she told her ugly daughter to lie on the side where she had no eye, and then the king wouldn't notice.

That evening when the king came home and heard that he had a baby son, he was delighted, and rushed to his dear wife's bedside to see how she was.

But the old witch quickly cried, "Don't draw back the curtains! The queen needs to rest."

So the king went away, unaware that it was not his real queen in the bed.

At midnight, when everyone else was asleep, the nursemaid sitting by the cradle in the nursery saw the door open and the real queen come into the room. She took the baby out of the cradle, held him in her arms, and gave him milk to drink. Then she shook his pillows out, laid him back on them, and put his little coverlet over him. She did not forget the little deer, either, going to the corner where he lay to stroke his back. Then she left without saying a word.

The next morning the nursemaid asked the guards if anyone had come into the castle during the night.

"No, we didn't see a soul," they replied.

The real queen came back night after night, and never said a word. The nursemaid always saw her, but she dared not tell anyone.

One night some time later, the real queen spoke in the night: "How is my child? How is my deer? Twice but no more will I come here."

The nursemaid did not reply, but when the queen had gone again, she went to the king and told him everything.

"What can this mean?" said the king. "I will keep watch by the baby myself tomorrow night."

The next evening he went to the nursery. The queen appeared again at midnight, and said: "How is my child? How is my deer? Once but no more will I come here."

Then she tended the child as usual before she disappeared. The king dared not speak to her, but he kept watch the next night too. This time the queen said, "How is my child? How is my deer? Never again will I come here."

The king could restrain himself no longer. He ran to her, saying, "You must be my dear wife!"

"Yes, I am indeed your dear wife," she said, and at that moment she came back to life, all rosy cheeked and healthy again. Then she told the king the dreadful thing the wicked witch and her daughter had done to her.

The king had them both brought to trial, and sentence was passed on them. The witch's daughter was taken into the forest, where wild beasts tore her to pieces, and the witch was burned to death on a bonfire. When there was nothing left of her but ashes, the spell on the little deer was broken, and he returned to human shape.

So Little Brother and Little Sister lived together happily for the rest of their lives.

BROWNELL LIBRARY

HOME OF

LITTLE COMPTON

FREE PUBLIC LIBRARY